Florence Parry Heide & Roxanne Heide Pierce

Always Listen
to Your
MOTHER

Illustrated by
Kyle M. Stone

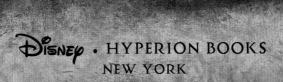

𝒟ISNEP • HYPERION BOOKS
NEW YORK

Errrrrrrrrnest?

"Yes, Mother?"

ONCE UPON A TIME there was
a nice little boy named Ernest.

Ernest always listened to
his mother. Nice little children
always listen to their mothers.

Ernest always:
played quietly, went to
bed on time, picked up
his toys, ate all his
vegetables, sat up
straight, and listened to
his mother.

Ernest never:
spilled, whined,
dawdled, talked back,
got his own way . . .

or had a good time.

Ernest's mother always:
swept, dusted, polished,
scrubbed, vacuumed,
mended, washed, ironed,
shined, polished, and cooked.

And Ernest always helped her.

Nice little children always help their mothers.

This is what his mother always said:

"It takes a lot of work to make a house a home."

One day Ernest looked out the window. A new family was moving into the house next door.

Ernest said, "There's a new family next door. Maybe there is someone I could play with. May I go over?"

Nice little children always ask their mothers if they may do something.

Otherwise,
they don't do it.

Ernest's mother said yes.
Mothers always want their children
to meet other nice children.

They want their children to meet nice
children who will be a good influence.

Ernest went next door
to meet the new neighbors.

"My name is Ernest," said Ernest.
"I live next door."

"My name is Vlapid," said Vlapid.
"And this is my mother."

"You look like the kind of boy
who always listens to his mother,"
said Vlapid's mother.

And of course she was right.

"You're welcome to stay for a while," said Vlapid's mother. "But you'll have to help. Here's a list of what needs to be done. It takes work to make a house a home."

And she went upstairs to have a mud bath.

This is what the list said:

Kitchen

Dining
room

Living
room

This is what Ernest
and Vlapid did:

Dining room

Vlapid's mother came downstairs. She looked around the house. "This is just the way I like things," she said.

When Ernest came home, he said, "There's someone my age in the new family next door and his name is Vlapid and he always listens to his mother."

"He sounds like a nice little boy," said Ernest's mother.

"He'll be a very good influence on you. I want you to play with him every day."

And Ernest did.

After all, nice little children
always listen to their mothers.

E
Heide

MAR   2011

$16.00

To Richard and Robert Heim and their parents, Jenny and John

—F.P.H. & R.H.P.

For Tamson— You're as good a friend
as you are an editor. Thank you.

—K.M.S.

First Edition
10 9 8 7 6 5 4 3 2 1
F850-6835-5-10105
Printed in Singapore
ISBN 978-1-4231-1395-9

Library of Congress Cataloging-in-Publication Data on file.
Visit www.hyperionbooksforchildren.com